ACADEMY OF THE SACRED HEART

NEW ORLEANS

PRESENTED BY

Nina Waring

August 30, 1997

Grandpa's House

Harvey Stevenson

Hyperion Books for Children
New York

For Josie, Pop, and Chelsea

Text and illustrations © 1994 by Harvey Stevenson.
All rights reserved. Printed in Hong Kong.
For information address Hyperion Books for Children,
114 Fifth Avenue, New York, New York 10011.

FIRST EDITION

1 3 5 7 9 10 8 6 4 2

Library of Congress Cataloging-in-Publication Data

Stevenson, Harvey.
Grandpa's house/Harvey Stevenson—1st ed.   p.   cm.
Summary: Grandpa is full of surprises for his young grandson Woody
who comes to visit him one summer weekend.
ISBN 1-56282-588-7 (trade)—ISBN 1-56282-589-5 (lib. bdg.)
[1. Grandfathers—Fiction.]   I. Title.
PZ7.S84745Gr   1994 [E]—dc20
93-6318 CIP AC

The artwork for each picture is prepared using
watercolor and pen and ink.
This book is set in 16-point Schneidler Medium.

Grandpa's House

Tomorrow, Woody and his parents are taking a plane to go to
Grandpa's house.
"Ready for takeoff...eerrrr...ffwooosh!" says Woody.
"Please try to go to sleep now," says Papa. But Woody is too excited
to sleep.
"Ffwooosh...," whispers Woody.

The taxi comes early in the morning. Mama and Papa carry all the bags.

"I forgot what Grandpa's like," says Woody.

"He likes to be barefoot, and he loves ice cream," says Papa.

"Yummm!" says Woody.

"And he's got a big tummy," says Mama.

"Me, too!" says Woody.

At the airport, Papa shows Woody all the different planes. "That one is very old, and that one is really fast, and we're going to take this big round one."

"Like Grandpa!" says Woody.

"Are we almost there yet?" Woody asks later, after the plane takes off.

"If you take a nap, we'll be there when you wake up," says Mama.

"Grandpa doesn't have to take a nap," says Woody.

"Grandpa *loves* naps," says Mama.

Woody gets off the plane and hops onto the baggage cart. From up there he can see Grandpa. He does have a big tummy! And he has a big mustache, too!

"Hiya, Peanut," says Grandpa.
"Your mustache tickles!" laughs Woody.
"So does yours!" says Grandpa.
"I don't have a mustache!" says Woody.
"Oops, where'd it go? Oh, never mind,"
says Grandpa.

Grandpa has a huge car and a dog named Eggroll. Eggroll's nice.
She gets to sit up front with Woody. "Pull my finger," says Grandpa,
and down the roof goes with a buzz.
"Wow," says Woody, "can I try?"
Mama and Papa fall asleep in the back. Grandpa, Woody, and Eggroll
stop for ice cream, but "only if we whisper!"

Grandpa always leaves all the doors and windows open at his house.
"Off with your shoes, Peanut!" says Grandpa. "No shoes allowed on
this vacation!"
"Bye, shoes," says Woody. "Hello, toes. Hello, grass. Hello, sand.
Hello, wet."

Then they follow a shady path down to the water. When Grandpa
flips the canoe over, spiders go scurrying away. Woody sits in front as
Grandpa slides the canoe into the warm water. Grandpa paddles
quietly along the reeds and out to a sandbar, where seagulls flap
away and leave their tracks in the mud.
"Woody's island."
"My island?" asks Woody, smiling.
"It's a sandbar that goes away and then
always comes back again, just
like you do," says Grandpa.

The next morning, Woody wakes up very early. He watches Grandpa steam up the mirror and make coffee right there in the bathroom sink. Clink goes the spoonful of coffee dropping into his mug.

"Look, magic!" says Grandpa, adding h water straight from the tap. The water becomes dark brown and smells strong "Mmm," says Grandpa.
"Yick!" says Woody.

"Shhhh," says Grandpa, "Mama and Papa are still asleep."

"Why are you crawling, Grandpa?" asks Woody.

"This is how Eggroll walks, and she's the quietest of all!" says Grandpa. "Hop on, Peanut!"

Woody rides Grandpa to the car.
Then off they go for a spin.
"Where're we going, Grandpa?" asks Woody.
"Time for supper, Peanut!"
"Not supper," laughs Woody.
"What, you're not hungry?"
"Breakfast!"
"Oh yes, of course, just what I said, breakfast,"
answers Grandpa, smiling.

They stop at Pete's Diner.
"Pancakes all around!" says Grandpa.
"For Eggroll, too?"
"Of course," says Grandpa.

On the way home, Grandpa shows Woody where the pigs live.
"Those are *horses*, Grandpa!" says Woody.
"Ah, so they are," says Grandpa.

"And hey, look at that cute little rabbit, Peanut!"
"That's a *turtle*, Grandpa!" says Woody.
"I suppose, on second thought…," says Grandpa,
tickling Woody's tummy.
"Looks like you!" says Woody.
"Beg your pardon?" says Grandpa.

When they get home, Woody follows Grandpa up the path to pick raspberries. There are tons of them, and they taste sweet; Woody's fingers turn red.

"Hey, save some of those bananas for me, will ya, Peanut?"

Woody smiles and then notices something in the grass.

"Snake, Grandpa!" Grandpa jumps, and Woody, laughing, pulls out the watering hose and runs down the path.

Woody decides to water the garden and discovers where Nini the cat
has been hiding. He waters the flowers and the bushes and the grass
and the bricks...and Grandpa!
"Hmm, looks like rain," says Grandpa.
Mama and Papa wake up and smile down from the balcony in the
morning light.

Woody helps Grandpa hang the wet things out to dry.
"Ouch! Hmm, I thought I felt one of those pesky alligators again,
Peanut. Did you see him?" asks Grandpa.
"Nope, must have gotten away," says Woody.
Under the peach tree the fallen peaches are warm and go *squish* under
Woody's feet.

Later, Grandpa builds Woody a tent as Mama and Papa
prepare dinner and talk with Woody's aunts and
uncles who've come to visit.

"And for dessert we'll have ice cream," says Grandpa.

"Yay! Strawberry?"

"No...mustard...," answers Grandpa, "or mud ice cream!"

"No...worm ice cream!" laughs Woody.

"How about some corn off the cob, Peanut?" asks Grandpa at dinner.

"Corn *on* the cob!" says Woody.

"Not if I can help it!" crunches Grandpa.

Woody gets to stay up late as everyone talks and laughs.

Woody wakes up in the night to hear thunder and the wind howling through the windows.
The porch door goes *tap, tap, tap.*

Wet spiderwebs stick to the window screens, and Woody decides to climb into Grandpa's bed.

In the morning everything is quiet. Fallen leaves are everywhere, and Grandpa is nowhere to be found. Woody discovers him sitting in the car with Eggroll.

"Whatcha doing, Grandpa?" asks Woody.

"Waiting...."

"For what?" asks Woody.

"For you!" says Grandpa. "Off we go to the beach!"

"Yay!" says Woody.

After the night's rain the beach is empty and beautiful and the ocean
is calm.

"Come ride on a whale, Peanut!" shouts Grandpa.

"You're no whale," says Woody.

"Right you are—only crabs make bubbles like this!"

"Crabs don't have mustaches," says Woody.

Grandpa and Woody make a giant plane in the sand.
"Ffwooosh...," says Woody.
"So long, Peanut!" says Grandpa.
"Bye, Grandpa!" Woody waves.

Grandpa takes Woody in his arms and gives him a soft poke in the
tummy. The sand is hot, and it's time for lunch. They walk back up
the beach toward the car.

"Do I have to go back tomorrow, Grandpa? I want to stay here,"
says Woody.

"If you stayed here all the time, you'd miss your home," says
Grandpa. "And it's the going away that makes it fun to come back."

That evening, Mama and Papa pack the bags. Woody sits with Grandpa and Eggroll and looks at books. Eggroll is warm against Woody's feet.

The next morning it's time to leave. Mama and Papa
feel a little bit sad, but now Woody's excited about
taking the plane again. Mama and Papa kiss
Grandpa good-bye. Woody runs into Grandpa's arms.
"Thanks, Grandpa, see you later....Ouch!"
Woody giggles. "Those pesky alligators again!"

"Bye, Eggroll! Bye, Grandpa! See you next time!"
"Don't forget to bring your mustache," says Grandpa.
"I don't have a mustache," says Woody, laughing.
"What? Hey! Where'd it go now? Oh, never mind," smiles Grandpa.